B R

MIDLOTHIA ...ement to concen... ...g. She is the author of a number of books for children, including *The Curse of the Skull, Emmelina and the Monster, No Tights for George!* and *Tarquin the Wonder Horse,* as well as several picture books for younger children. A frequent visitor to primary schools to give readings, talks and workshops, June lives in Leicestershire, where she enjoys horse-riding as often as possible!

Books by the same author

Jumping Beany

June Crebbin

WALKER BOOKS
AND SUBSIDIARIES

LONDON • BOSTON • SYDNEY • AUCKLAND

First published 2004 by Walker Books Ltd
87 Vauxhall Walk, London SE11 5HJ

2 4 6 8 10 9 7 5 3 1

Text © 2004 June Crebbin
Illustrations © 2004 David Roberts

The right of June Crebbin to be identified as author
of this work has been asserted by her in accordance
with the Copyright, Designs and Patents Act 1988

This book has been typeset in Stempel Schneidler

Printed in Great Britain by J.H. Haynes & Co. Ltd

British Library Cataloguing in Publication Data:
a catalogue record for this book
is available from the British Library

ISBN 0-7445-8382-9

www.walkerbooks.co.uk

*For Esmé, Georgie, Holly, Jess,
Josh, Lara, Lucy and Sammy*

With special thanks to Gail

Amber stamped upstairs in her riding boots.

"Mum!" she yelled. "We're going to be late."

"No, we're not," Mum called from the bathroom. "I'm just changing Sam's nappy."

Amber groaned. She desperately wanted to ride Beany this week, the last chance she'd get before Pony Day next week. Amber loved Pony Days when she spent all day at the stables, riding, and learning how to look after her favourite pony, Beany – if she was lucky. Dad had set her the challenge of winning the jumping competition this time, and what's more he was going to be there to see her do it. Being a stuntman, doing amazing things all over the world, kept him away from home so often he'd always missed Amber's Pony Days before.

Amber thought she could do it, but she needed Beany. He was so eager, so keen to have a go. She knew he loved jumping as much as she did. They were a team.

Unfortunately, Donna liked riding Beany too.

The clock downstairs in the living-room chimed ten ringing notes.

"Mum!" shouted Amber, whacking the bannister with her riding whip. "It's ten o'clock!"

"No, it isn't," said Mum, coming out of the bathroom. "That clock's fast." She hoisted Sam onto one hip.

"How fast?" asked Amber as they went downstairs.

"Oh, at least five minutes," said Mum.

"Is Lily ready?"

Amber nodded. Lily was always on time.

"Have you seen my car keys?" said Mum.

Amber held back a groan. "Where did you put them?" she asked.

"I don't know," said Mum. "If I knew that, I wouldn't be asking, would I?"

She dumped Sam in his high chair and rummaged through the piles of newspapers and magazines on the kitchen table.

"Why don't you get a hook?" snapped Amber, peering into saucepans and opening drawers. Other people, sensible people, hung keys on hooks as they walked into the house and picked them up off hooks as they walked out. Like Molly's mum. She had a whole row of hooks by the back door, each labelled with its function – CAR, GARAGE, BACK DOOR, CELLAR. Very sensible.

"They're not here," said Amber. She marched into the living-room. Lily was sitting on the edge of the sofa clutching her dancing case.

"Is Mum ready?" she asked anxiously. "I don't like being late."

Amber snorted. She tipped her younger sister off the sofa to search under the cushions. "You're not the only one!" she said. No keys.

Amber worked her way swiftly round the room, lifting cushions, up-ending ornaments, even rooting around the toy-box. She knew from experience her mum's keys could be anywhere.

Lily watched from her new position on the little wicker stool.

"You could help!" snapped Amber, shoving aside piles of carrier bags full of material waiting for Mum's attention.

"I can't," said Lily. "I'm only five." She screwed up her face.

"Don't you dare start crying," warned Amber. Once Lily switched on the floods, they'd never get away.

Floods!

Amber dived into the hall. It had been raining yesterday when Mum picked them up from school. Mum's waterproof jacket was on its hook. Amber dug into the pockets.

"Found them!" she called.

"Where?" said Mum.

"In your jacket!" said Amber.

They piled into the car.

"Help Lily," said Mum.

"I can do it on my own," said Lily, snapping her seat belt shut.

"We're still late," Amber hissed.

Too late to ride Beany. Donna would be riding him by now.

"Donna's riding Beany today," said Carol at the stables, as she took Amber's money and crossed her name off the list.

"But Donna rode Beany last week," said Amber.

"You're riding Minnie," said Carol.

Amber scowled. "Minnie!" she said. "You're kidding. Minnie's hopeless. She keeps stopping."

"Well, I'm sorry," said Carol. "But your lesson started ten minutes ago. Donna was here on time, and she asked for Beany."

She would, thought Amber bitterly.

Donna showed off on Beany, prancing about, winding him up. He didn't need it.

"Can I have Jester?" said Amber.

"No, Jack's riding Jester," said Carol.

"Why?" asked Amber. Jack always rode Rocket Roger. He and Rocket Roger were like – well, like fruit and nut, cod and chips, chocolate and mint ice cream.

"Roger has a sore foot," said Carol.

"What about Polka?" suggested Amber.

"Lydia's riding Polka," said Carol.

"But Lydia's got two ponies of her own!" cried Amber. "Even if one is a lead-rein pony, she could at least bring the other one to ride."

"I'm sure she will," said Carol. "But not today. Now stop asking questions and let's get you on board."

The phone rang. Carol picked it up. "Merryfield Hall Riding School," she said. "How can I help you?"

Amber muttered under her breath. She

wasn't getting much help.

She went over to the window. Outside was the big square courtyard of the old stables that had been built with Merryfield Hall over a hundred years ago. Nowadays, horses at livery were kept there but Amber liked to imagine horses and carriages sweeping up the long winding drive through the woods and parkland to the Hall.

The Hall was a hotel now, a very posh one. People paid a lot of money to stay, or have weddings or parties there. Children from the riding school were not allowed anywhere near.

But Amber had been inside once. Mum had made a bride's gown, and when she'd gone to deliver it the night before the wedding, had taken Amber with her. Amber had never seen such an amazing place. Huge banqueting rooms, marble pillars, glittering chandeliers, and a magnificent red and gold ballroom.

Lily would be going there on the same day as Amber's Pony Day. Her dancing teacher was getting married, and all the children were giving the bride a special performance.

Carol put the phone down. "Let's go," she said.

Amber followed her down the path to the riding school. There were big airy stables for the horses and smaller stalls for the ponies. There was a tack room and a wash-box, a large indoor arena and beyond that an outdoor manège.

Minnie was waiting in her stall, tacked up and ready. Amber led her to the indoor arena, scowling when she saw that Donna was leading the ride. Beany looked lovely, ears pricked, feet stepping out briskly, tail swishing just the way it should.

Amber, aware of everyone watching her, mounted Minnie and joined the end of the ride.

Three

"Nice to see you, Amber," said Jen, their riding instructor. "Now keep Minnie moving. You know how she likes to go to sleep."

Molly, in front of her, on Feather as usual, twisted round in her saddle. "We thought you weren't coming," she said. "Donna's riding Beany."

"I can see that," snapped Amber.

Molly looked crushed. "I only meant…"

"Sitting trot, everyone," called Jen. "Think about spacing. Don't get too close." Amber urged Minnie forwards. Feather was old and gentle, which is why Molly stuck to him, but he could still get a move on when he felt like it. Amber wanted to keep up.

"When are we going to jump?" called Donna.

"Can we canter?" said Lydia.

"All in good time," said Jen. "Now back to walk. We'll have two circles."

"Can we have teams?" said Donna.

"Oh," said Molly. "I'm no good at teams."

"Jack, you lead off the second circle," said Jen.

"Can we choose names?" said Jack, standing up in his stirrups. "We'll be the Winners!"

"More like the Wimps!" jeered Donna.

"So, forward into rising trot, Jack and Donna," called Jen. "And sit and – canter!"

Each rider cantered round to the end of the ride. Then they all cantered at the same time. Jen gave marks for spacing and rhythm.

"You're bound to win," yelled Jack. "You've got the best ponies."

"What's your team called?" shouted Lydia.

"We're the Stars!" yelled Donna, flying round on Beany.

"Hurry up, Amber!" shouted Jack, fast catching up with Minnie, who had still not launched herself into canter despite Amber's best efforts.

"Sit down in the saddle, Amber," said Jen. "Slide your leg back and nudge Minnie's side firmly. Let her know you mean business."

At last Minnie consented to canter and Amber worked hard to keep her going.

"What are our scores?" called Lydia.

"I think…" said Jen. "I think – 9 to the Stars, because your spacing is extra good today and … 8 to the Winners!"

"No, the Wimps!" yelled Donna.

"No, the Whoopsies!" said Jen, as Jester stopped abruptly to deposit large dollops right in front of Feather.

"Everyone back to walk," said Jen. "Now

we'll practise our figures of eight. It'll help you for your jumping competition next week. Is everyone coming?"

Amber held her breath. Perhaps Donna was going on holiday for half-term. Maybe she was off to pose with penguins in Antarctica or preen with parrots in South America. She was always going somewhere far and fancy.

Sure enough.

"We're going to be sailing our yacht round the Greek islands," said Donna.

Amber grinned.

"But we're coming back specially for Pony Day," finished Donna.

Amber groaned.

Jen was setting up the jumps, a course of three to start with, cross poles, a straight and a spread. There were two poles on the spread, one slightly in front of the other. "I'll put fillers under them," said Jen. "It's more fun."

Molly looked anxiously at the colourful

striped boards Jen was hooking beneath the poles.

"Does Feather like fillers?" asked Molly.

"He'll be fine," said Jen.

Everyone jumped in turn. Amber kept her legs close to Minnie's sides, urging her forward and although Minnie plodded round, she didn't stop.

"Well done," said Jen. "That's really good, Amber."

"But can I ride Beany on Pony Day?" asked Amber.

"Will Rocket Roger be better by then?" asked Jack. "Time will count, won't it?"

"I am riding Feather, aren't I?" said Molly.

"We'll sort out ponies later," said Jen. "Now we'll add a double."

She paced out the strides between the two jumps of the double. "You'll have room for a couple of strides," she said. "Keep your ponies straight and remember to urge them on between the jumps."

After the lesson, everyone met at the office.

"Can I ride Beany?" said Amber.

"Surely I should ride him," said Donna. "After all, I have been practising on him today."

"You could have Polka," said Jen.

"What about Lydia?" said Donna.

"I'm bringing Supersonic Silver," said Lydia. "He's really fast."

"Faster than Beany?" said Donna. "I don't think so."

"Polka can move," said Jen. "You've ridden him before."

Donna pulled a face. "But I prefer Beany," she said. "Why can't Amber have Polka?"

"Because it's only fair to take turns," said Jen. "Amber likes Beany too."

"Yes, but she'll be riding him all day," said Donna. "Not just a lesson."

"We'll remember it's your turn next Pony Day," said Jen. "I promise."

"I still don't think it's fair," said Donna.

Jen had heard enough. "It's Polka or nothing, Donna," she said. "It's up to you."

Donna glared.

"Well?" said Jen.

Donna shrugged her shoulders. "Polka, I suppose."

She flounced out of the door.

Jen had a quiet word with Amber as the others left. "I know you like riding Beany," she said, "and it's only fair you and Donna take turns. But these days we never know whether you're coming or not." She smiled. "Better make sure you're on time for Pony Day."

Amber nodded. Her insides were turning somersaults with excitement. She just mustn't be late. Somehow she had to get her mum organized. Nothing was going to stop her from jumping Beany.

All week Amber longed for Pony Day. When it came, she leapt out of bed at six o'clock to zap the button on her alarm clock and rushed to the window. Perfect. There was that lovely haze that promised a really hot day.

She tiptoed downstairs. First, she'd set out the breakfast things and make her packed lunch. Then she'd wake Lily and take Mum a cup of tea. That would leave plenty of time for Mum to see to Sam. Everything about Sam took ages – feeding, bathing, changing. Today, Amber was allowing for it, but just to make sure, she had a master plan:

the living-room clock.

Pony Day started at nine. If she put the clock forward an hour, so that it chimed nine ringing notes when really it was only eight, they were bound to be on time.

Amber decided to alter the clock first. Carefully, she eased the living-room door open so it wouldn't creak – and trod softly across the carpet. The clock was very old. It had been given to Amber's great-grand-mother on her wedding day way back at the beginning of the last century. Amber wasn't supposed to touch it. But today she was desperate. Gently, she opened the front casing and laid her finger against the minute hand. She began to move it slowly, slowly—

"What on earth do you think you're doing?" said a voice from the other side of the room.

Amber's finger skidded across the clock's face. The clock lurched backwards and jangled madly. Amber put out both hands to steady it. Mum appeared at her side and pushed her out of the way.

"It's stopped ticking," she said. "How many times have I told you…?"

"You made me jump!" said Amber. "I didn't know you were there." Her heart was still beating a wild jigaloo against her ribs.

The clock resumed its quiet ticking.

"You'd better explain," said Mum, going back to her sewing machine. "But I must get Lily's hat finished. The wedding's today, remember."

Amber took a deep breath. "It's very, very important to me that I'm on time at the stables today," she began, "so—"

"Well, you don't have to worry," Mum interrupted. "Molly and her mum are picking you up."

Amber felt indignant. "Nobody told me," she said.

"I'm picking Dad up from the airport," said Mum.

"Will he really be there to see me jump?" said Amber.

"Yes," said Mum. "Everything's arranged."

Amber crossed her fingers behind her back. She had heard that so many times before and then things had got muddled because Mum hadn't planned properly.

"What do you think?" said Mum. She held up the hat. It was like a pixie's cap, made up of petal-shaped pieces, gold, lime green and yellow.

Amber knew how to respond. "It's lovely," she said.

She went into the kitchen to make her sandwiches.

At least she could trust Molly's mum to be on time.

Molly and her mum were early. So early that when they arrived at the stables, Jen gave Molly and Amber a head-collar each and said they could help bring all the ponies in from the field.

"Oh, bliss! Oh, joy!" chanted Amber, as she walked down the lane, swinging the head-collar.

"Oh dear," said Molly. "I hope Feather's easy to catch."

None of the ponies was a problem. On the way back, Amber and Molly were allowed to ride bareback once they were off the main street.

Donna passed them as they neared the yard and made a rude face through the back window of the car.

"Did you see that?" gasped Molly.

Amber smiled serenely. "Doesn't bother me," she said.

There were fifteen people altogether on the Pony Day. Although their ages varied and some of them had lessons at a different time from Amber's during the week, they were all about the same ability.

First, they learnt about stable management. They had to groom their ponies and pick their feet out. Then they practised tying lead-ropes. "Just to remind you," said Jen. "It's your responsibility after each riding session to secure your pony safely." She inspected each pony. Lydia had forgotten to tuck the end of the rope through the loop, which meant that Silver could have pulled it undone.

"You'd have come back from lunch," said

Jen, "and Supersonic Silver would have been in the next county!"

"It's a quick release knot for us, not for the pony, isn't it?" said Donna.

"Know-it-all," Lydia muttered under her breath. Amber grinned.

Then they tacked up, and at last it was time to ride.

Beany was full of beans during the warm-up. That's how he'd got his name, Jen had once told them! He'd been full of life ever since she'd known him. Amber relaxed in the saddle and went with him. She loved his eagerness, the way she never had to bully him into trot or canter like she did with Minnie.

She was glad to be at the front of the ride, well away from Donna, but when it came to "pairs", they were chosen to ride together.

"I want to see a nice brisk walk," said Jen. "Get your ponies stepping under you."

Donna was riding on the outside.

"Keep together," said Jen. "Inside ones slower round the corners, outside ones getting a move on."

Amber was ready for Donna, but even so, Donna scooted so fast round the first corner, she and Beany were left behind.

"Oh, did I lose you?" said Donna. "So sorry."

Amber scowled. Of course, at the next corner, Donna went really slowly and Amber ended up way ahead.

"You two can do better than that," said Jen.

Amber was glad when the session finished. She hated messing Beany about. But she needn't have worried about upsetting him. After a break, they practised the course they would be jumping in the competition that afternoon. Beany jumped flawlessly. Polka on the other hand rushed his fences, clipped a couple with his back legs, bringing them down, and ran out at the spread.

Donna wrenched him round.

"Stupid, stupid pony!" she cried, hitting him with her whip.

"If you do that again," said Jen, "you can dismount, unless Polka bucks you off first. I wouldn't blame him. You're pushing him on much too fast. Take your time. Try again."

After Donna had thumped her heels into Polka's sides and cleared the jump, everyone went to lunch in the big field behind the stables.

Amber sat well away from Donna during lunch and was pleased to see her going off somewhere after they'd eaten. Amber and Molly sat in the sunshine making daisy chains and watching the big horses moving lazily about the meadow below them.

Every so often, snatches of music drifted towards them. Maybe it's coming from the wedding, thought Amber. She wondered if Mum had taken Lily yet. Being where she should be on time wasn't her mum's strong point. Then there was meeting Dad at the airport. Amber just hoped Mum would make it.

"Let's go back to the stables," said Amber, jumping up suddenly. "Come on. I want to see Beany."

"We're not allowed," protested Molly, but she followed her all the same.

"Where are you two going?" called the girl in charge.

"Toilet," yelled Amber.

"OK. Come straight back."

The stables were quiet. Most of the horses were out in the fields. Ponies were giving full attention to their hay-nets.

Amber and Molly walked past them – Jester, Polka, Supersonic Silver, Roger and in the very last stall, Beany.

Except that Beany wasn't there.

His stall was empty.

"Looking for Beany?" said Donna, appearing round the edge of the building. "Oh, dear, has he gone missing?"

"What have you done with him?" said Amber.

"Me?" said Donna, all wide-eyed with innocence. "As if."

"I'm going to tell Jen," said Amber.

"I wouldn't if I were you," said Donna. "She'll only think you forgot to tie him up properly."

"That's a lie!" said Amber.

"Well, he must have got out somehow," said Donna, smirking. "Oh dear, you can't jump in the competition now, can you? What a shame." And she sauntered off.

Molly gasped. "What are you going to do?"

"We," said Amber, "are going to find him."

Molly was horrified. "How?"

"Look for him, of course," said Amber.

Molly didn't move. "We should tell Carol," she said. "She'll know what to do."

"NO!" said Amber. "There isn't time. He must be somewhere in the grounds of Merryfield Hall. Even Donna wouldn't turn him out onto the road. We could find him and have him back before anyone notices if we go now."

She marched off up the drive. "You search that side, and I'll search this. Yell as soon as you see him. If you don't find him, meet at the Hall gates."

"I don't think—" began Molly.

"GO ON!" shouted Amber. She disappeared into the trees.

Paths veered off in all directions. Some of them led to clearings where there were stone statues and seats to allow guests to rest or admire the view.

Amber hurried frantically in and out of the trees.

No sign of Beany.

Now and then, she made herself stop and listen, hoping she might hear Beany munching or moving about. But there was only birdsong and the occasional squirrel rustling about.

By the time she met up with Molly at the Hall gates, she was feeling desperate.

"Nothing," she said. "What about you?"

Molly shook her head. "I didn't see him," she said. "I'd have yelled – there he is!"

Amber turned back. "We'll have to search again," she said.

Molly grabbed her arm. "No, no," she cried, waving her arms wildly. "I mean – THERE HE IS!"

Amber looked. In front of the hotel, beautifully tended lawns led down to a lake. Close by the lake was Beany, quietly cropping the grass, his lead-rope trailing behind him.

"Quick, let's get him!" yelled Molly.

"No, wait!" cried Amber. Beyond Beany, the wedding reception was in full swing, all the guests seated at a circle of tables, waiters milling about with loaded trays.

The last thing Amber wanted was to get anywhere near the wedding. If someone recognized her, she'd be in even bigger trouble.

But Molly was on a mission. "Beany!" she called, sprinting across the grass. "BEANY!"

Amber set off hotfoot behind her. Maybe she could overtake Molly, stop her from frightening Beany into flight. They should be approaching him quietly, not charging at him like bulls to a red rag.

Suddenly, Beany's head jerked up; he saw

Molly racing towards him, arms waving, yelling, and took off – straight towards the wedding.

Molly stopped.

Beany galloped on.

A waiter, becoming aware of Beany's approach, shouted a warning.

People screamed as Beany flew closer, and fled from their seats.

Beany, finding his way blocked by tables, leapt into the air, soared over them and landed, only to find himself trapped on all sides.

He stopped, quivering, uncertain what to do. Then he lowered his head and began to graze, keeping a watchful eye on proceedings.

The crowd quietened, waiting to see what would happen as Molly and Amber arrived.

"Stay here, Molly," Amber whispered fiercely.

She eased her way between the tables

towards Beany.

"Steady, boy," she called soothingly. "It's only me." She felt in her pocket for the titbits she always carried. "Come on, beautiful. Look what I've brought you." She held out her hand.

Beany raised his head, stretched his neck towards her and sniffed cautiously. As he bent his head to accept the offering, Amber quietly grabbed his lead-rope.

Some of the crowd clapped. Some even cheered. But not everyone.

"What a mess!" cried a woman in a purple dress with a huge purple hat and feather to match. "Are you responsible for this animal?"

Amber looked around. Plates and dishes and glasses lay scattered in the churned-up grass; chairs had been knocked over in the rush to get out of the way; some of the guests were dabbing at stains on their clothes where food and drink had been spilt.

She felt sick. "I'm so sorry," she said.

"Sorry!" said Purple Hat. "I think you'll have to do better than that, young lady. I'll be talking to your parents. They shouldn't allow you to have a pony if you can't control him."

"He isn't her pony!" shouted Molly. "He's from the riding school."

All eyes turned.

Oh, thanks, Molly, thought Amber. That's really done it. Now we'll be marched back to Jen, who will be absolutely appalled and we'll be banished from riding at Merryfield ever again.

She thought quickly. If she apologized again and promised to pay for the damage, maybe they'd be allowed to go. It would take weeks and weeks of her pocket money, she could see that, but it would be worth it. With luck, they'd still be in time for the jumping competition. If they left now.

"I'm really, really sorry," said Amber. "Of

course, I'll pay for the damage we've caused, but we do have to go." She began to lead Beany firmly towards the outside of the circle. A couple of waiters moved a table out of the way for her to pass.

"Stop!" shouted Purple Hat, turning purple. "Someone should go with her."

Amber's heart sank. If someone came back with them, there'd be explanations that would go on and on. Jen would want to know the whys and wherefores of Beany's escape. Donna would deny any knowledge of it. Amber would be blamed. Her parents would be called in – and as for the jumping competition, she might as well forget it.

"Just a minute," said a voice. The bride rose from her seat. "I'll deal with this, Mum," she said. She floated towards Amber.

"Aren't you Lily's sister?" she asked.

"Yes," said Amber. "But…"

"I thought I recognized you. I'm Angela. Lily's dancing teacher."

Amber nodded. "Yes, I know," she said. She tightened her grip on Beany's lead-rope. "I'm very, very sorry. We didn't mean to upset your wedding." Even as she carried on apologizing, she felt it was hopeless. After all, they had barged in and spoilt what was supposed to be a happy occasion. She didn't blame the bride for being angry and upset.

Suddenly Amber realized Angela was neither of these things. She wasn't even listening. She was putting out her hand to stroke Beany's neck.

"May I?" she said. "It is Beany, isn't it?"

"Who would have thought it?" said Molly, as she skipped happily along beside Amber and Beany back down the drive. "Fancy Angela knowing Beany!"

Amber nodded. She wished they could move faster. She'd have liked to gallop back to the stables.

"And she used to jump him," Molly went on. "At our riding school. Imagine!"

Amber hurried on. If only they could get back before the lunch hour was finished, before anyone noticed they were missing.

At least Angela had helped them get away, taking all responsibility, telling them not to worry about anything.

"It's lovely to see Beany again," she'd said. "He doesn't look any different and I noticed he's still good at jumping!"

She had delayed them slightly, insisting on having her photograph taken with Beany. "I'd love to watch you jump," she whispered to Amber as they left. "Good luck!"

I'll need it, thought Amber. I could kill Donna. But I'm going to keep calm. I am.

She pressed on. The drive seemed endless. The riding stables weren't even in sight yet.

"Wait!" cried Molly suddenly. "I can hear something."

"What?" said Amber, marching on.

"Crying," said Molly. "There's someone in the woods crying."

"Well, it's nothing to do with us," said Amber firmly.

Molly clutched her arm. "Suppose whoever's in there is hurt."

All Amber wanted to do was keep going.

Goodness knows they didn't need another delay. But she knew she couldn't.

"All right," she said. "You go first."

Molly led the way along a narrow path. Amber had to walk ahead of Beany but she kept tight hold of the lead-rope. The crying was getting louder. The path opened out into a clearing. In the middle was a stone seat and on the seat sat the strangest little figure.

Molly gasped. She stopped so abruptly that Amber bumped into her.

"What?" she said.

"It's a—" began Molly.

"What?" said Amber. She couldn't see a thing.

"Do you believe in fairies?" said Molly.

It was on the tip of Amber's tongue to say, No, of course not, but then she remembered that once, when she was little, she'd been told that every time someone said they didn't believe in fairies, a fairy died.

"I'm not sure," she said.

"Well, there's one in there," said Molly.

"Don't be silly," said Amber. She handed the lead-rope to Molly. "Let me see."

She peered round the edge of a rhododendron bush. The little figure, slightly turned away from her, sat cross-legged on the stone seat. It was dressed all in green and on its head was a hat like a pixie's cap made up of petal-pieces, gold, lime green and yellow.

"It is a fairy, isn't it?" said Molly, leaning forward. Beany took the opportunity to step backwards and grab a mouthful of leaves. A twig broke beneath his foot.

The figure on the stone seat turned towards them, tears streaming down its pale face.

Amber gasped.

"Lily!" she said.

Lily jumped off the seat, ran across the clearing and flung herself at Amber. She clung on tight, sobbing, her breath coming in gasps.

Amber prised her off and held her at arm's

length. "Stop it!" she said sharply. "Stop crying and tell me what's happened."

Lily cried even more and struggled to get her arms round Amber again. She was working herself up to fever pitch. Amber knew the signs.

Quickly, expertly, she moved Lily over to the seat, sat her down, and knelt in front of her. "Now," she said, "tell me what's happened."

Between huge gulps, Lily explained. It seemed that all the dancers who were dressed and ready had been allowed to sit outside in the sunshine with a snack. "I saw a squirrel," said Lily. "So I went over to give it some of my biscuit." She caught her breath. "But it ran off."

"And you ran after it?" said Amber.

Lily nodded.

"Then what happened?" said Amber.

"It disappeared," whispered Lily. "I was frightened."

"Of course you were," said Amber, "but you're fine now because I'm here and Molly's here – and Beany's here!"

She stood up and led Lily to where Molly and Beany were waiting. "So we'll all go back to the stables together."

Lily's face began to wobble. "I don't want to go to the stables," she said. "I want to do my dance for Angela."

"I know you do," agreed Amber, "and you will." But she felt mean even as she said it. She knew that by the time they reached the stables and Carol or someone had rung the hotel and made arrangements for Lily to be taken back, her part in the wedding would be over.

Amber looked at her sister. "Some pixie you are!" she said.

Lily's pale face was tear-streaked and dirty. Her pixie cap was askew. Her costume was less than clean.

"Are we going or not?" said Molly. Beany

was getting restless.

"You are," said Amber. "Tell Jen I had to take Lily to the wedding. Tell her everything. I'll be back as soon as I can."

"But you'll miss the competition!" said Molly.

"I know," said Amber.

Amber strode out along the drive, dragging Lily along with her.

"You're hurting my arm," wailed Lily. "You're going too fast."

"You want to get back in time, don't you?" snapped Amber.

Lily cried quietly.

Amber slowed down. "Sorry," she said.

It had been horrible seeing Molly and Beany going off in the opposite direction. Yet again Beany would be at the stables and she wouldn't. How Donna would love that! She'd deny all knowledge of Beany's escape of course. Then she'd offer to ride him.

Amber could just imagine it. "Well, I might as well," she'd say. "Amber isn't here."

A car overtook them and pulled in up ahead.

Even when Molly told Jen the truth about Beany's escape, thought Amber, it was only their word against Donna's. There was no proof.

A woman got out of the car. She waved frantically.

"Mum!" shouted Amber. "Come on, Lily. It's Mum!"

There was a flurry of explanations and hugs. Mum phoned the hotel to explain about Lily. "Yes, she's quite safe," Amber heard her say, "though I can't think how she managed to get so far on her own. If it hadn't been for my elder daughter... Yes, I'm bringing her right away." She gave Lily another hug. "We'll soon have you dancing with all the other pixies! I'll just phone the stables—"

"There's no need," interrupted Amber.

"Molly will tell them what's happened."

"But I'd like them to know you're on your way," said Mum.

Amber shrugged. "I'm not going," she said. "What's the point?"

She'd rather stay and watch pixies than arrive at the stables just in time to see Donna in a blaze of glory getting a clear round on Beany.

"But what about the jumping competition?" said Mum.

"It'll be too late," muttered Amber.

"Well," said Mum, dithering. "If I…"

"It's all right," said Amber. "I know you have to take Lily first."

Mum hesitated, then she opened the car door. "You and Lily get in," she said, "and I'll just give the stables a quick call. It'll only take a minute."

It wasn't until Amber strapped herself in that she realized the only other person in the car was Sam, fast asleep in the front.

"Where's Dad?" she demanded, as soon as Mum had finished phoning. "I thought you were going to meet him?"

"His plane was delayed," said Mum, as they drove off. She shot a swift glance at Amber. "I know he promised to be here, but there's nothing we can do about it."

Amber shrugged. "Doesn't matter," she said, staring out of the window. "I'm not jumping anyway."

When they reached the hotel car park, she was surprised to find Mum's friend Ann waiting, engine revving, ready to whisk her back to the stables.

"Off you go!" said Mum, giving her a hug.

"I don't want to," said Amber.

"Yes, you do," said Mum. "Good luck!"

Amber shrank into her seat. Why did grown-ups always think they knew best?

"You're having quite a day, aren't you?" said Ann, cheerfully.

Amber pretended not to hear.

Amber was delivered to the stables' office. Like a parcel, she thought. Carol, on the phone as usual, waved at Ann and mouthed "thank you". Amber summoned up enough politeness to offer her own thanks though she felt anything but gratitude. She was exhausted. She didn't want to explain anything to anyone ever again. But Jen would want her version of all the incidents. And she'd have things to say about her going off on her own. Amber wished she could just go home.

"Come on," said Carol, putting the phone down.

"I don't feel well," said Amber. She really didn't. Her insides were fluttery. Her throat ached.

"You'll be fine," said Carol. "I should think you'll be just in time."

For what? thought Amber. The gymkhana? They always finished Pony Days with a gymkhana – team races picking bean bags off sticks and throwing them into buckets, trotting up and cantering back, weaving in and out of cones, things like that. Amber just didn't feel up to it.

She followed Carol across to the riding school. She didn't want to ask but she found herself doing so anyway.

"Who won the jumping?" she said as casually as she could.

But Carol didn't hear. There was such a noise coming from the indoor arena. The gymkhana was indeed in progress. Everyone was cheering on their team. Molly was waiting in line on Feather. She saw Amber and waved madly. Then she did the thumbs-up sign, which was quite difficult considering she was holding the reins, and all the while she was grinning and nodding her head. Then it was her turn and she was off and away, riding one-handed, the other hand on her hat.

Jen saw Amber, and at the end of the race she handed over to one of the helpers and came over.

Here we go, thought Amber.

"Did Molly tell you…?" she began.

Amber hesitated. How much did Jen know?

It turned out Molly had told her about Beany going missing and their part in it, and Jen already knew about Donna's part because one of the helpers had seen Donna leading Beany down the yard.

"The silly girl said nothing," said Jen, "until we found not only Beany missing but you and Molly as well!"

Amber apologized for going off without telling anyone.

"Well," said Jen, "I've had strong words with Donna, and I think we should put the whole thing behind us. Are you up to the jumping competition?"

For a moment Amber was stunned. She couldn't think straight. Surely that was over.

Jen smiled. "Your mother told me all about your little sister being lost and you looking after her, even though it meant you missing the competition. So I've switched the last two events round. We're going to end with jumping today."

There was an enormous cheer behind them.

"Sounds as if the gymkhana's finishing," said Jen. "We'll have a quick break for drinks and then we'll get going. Beany's all tacked up ready, but perhaps you'd like to go outside and remind yourself of the course. We've all done that. See you in a minute or two."

Amber walked out into the sunshine in a daze. One minute you thought all was lost and nothing would ever be right again. Then, the next, everything was turned upside down and the possibilities were endless.

She opened the gate into the outdoor manège. It was very hot. In the distance, on the other side of the blue flax field, riders crested the hill; along the lane, trees barely shifted in the still air; above, in a sea-blue sky, a small aeroplane buzzed lazily.

Perfect. Everything was perfect. Well, almost, Amber thought. If only Dad could have been there.

Amber began to walk the course. All the numbers had been put clearly in place. Number 1, a cross poles; Number 2, a straight and then she would have to keep well out around the corner to approach another straight at Number 3. Very straightforward! She grinned.

Then a big swing out behind the first

fence, remembering to change leg to approach Number 4, a spread with shark's teeth fillers. Oooh, could be spooky, those boards with the zig-zag black and white patterns! She'd have to make sure she lined Beany up really well so he'd get a good look at it. She retraced her steps to check and became aware of the aeroplane again. It seemed to be circling over the fields to her left, over the big field where they'd eaten their lunch.

When she looked up again, after Number 5, the planks, and Numbers 6a and 6b, the double, usually no trouble as long as she kept Beany balanced for the two strides in between, she saw that the aeroplane was moving away, leaving behind ... a falling figure!

Amber gasped, but at that moment a parachute ballooned above the figure, and it began a gentle, swinging descent to the ground.

Amazing! Why would a parachutist be landing at their riding school? Maybe it was a late guest for the wedding arriving a bit off course!

She turned her mind back to the jumps. The others would be out soon. Number 7, the rustic gate, and lastly, Number 8, the parallel. A really tricky one. She'd have to be careful with that one. It was all too easy to lose concentration on the last fence and knock off a rail.

"Amber!"

Amber looked round. It must be time to start. But she couldn't see anyone calling her from the stables.

"Amber!" The shout came again. The voice was coming from behind her.

She turned.

"Dad!" she yelled.

Her father was standing in the next field, calmly rolling up his parachute.

Amber climbed over the fence and ran to meet him.

"Just thought I'd drop in!" he said, as she arrived. "Have I missed anything?"

Amber took Beany over the practice jump for a second time. He felt good. He was on his toes, but she didn't mind that. He was listening, that's what mattered. She'd walked, trotted and cantered him in the warm-up and he was doing everything she asked.

Amber felt sick with excitement. She tried to relax. It was no use getting too worked up. That would just put Beany on edge, and then he'd rush and be careless. She thrust her heels well down in their stirrups and made herself breathe deeply.

The bell rang. First to jump was Lydia. Silver

was really keen, prancing about as Lydia steered him towards the start. Lydia did well to hold him as she put him into canter for the first jump. But she held him all the way and they finished clear. The competition had two rounds. In the first, the aim was to jump clear. Then, if you did that, you were in the "jump-off", which meant you jumped fewer, slightly higher fences but this time against the clock – the fastest clear round won!

Next to jump was Jack on Roger, who rocketed round as usual, catching one of the rails on the last jump, which rolled in its cups and nearly fell, causing the spectators to draw in their breath sharply and let it out again as the rail settled back into place. Another clear round!

"I don't mind Feather being slow," said Molly. "I just want to do a clear round."

And she did.

Donna was next on Polka. She looked very grim, thought Amber, very determined, but then she never was a bundle of laughs. Donna rode Polka hard at every fence, thumping him over, then wrenching him round ready for the next jump. Amber felt sorry for him. Minnie needed strong encouragement as did Feather but Polka was a willing soul most of the time. Still, it was another clear round, so obviously Donna knew what she was doing.

Then there was a boy on Jester and two girls who all jumped clear. Last to jump was Amber. She kept Beany nice and steady. No point going for speed at this stage, and although Beany quickened his pace considerably heading towards the spread with the shark's teeth fillers, he sailed over it, no trouble, and on safely to the last.

They were in the jump-off!

There were eight clears altogether.

"I can't believe it! I can't believe it!" Molly kept saying as they all put their ponies away. Jen wanted just the riders in the arena so that she could explain the shortened course.

"You need to jump Numbers 1 to 5," she said. "They're slightly higher, but you can all do them, and of course this time you need to get a move on." She smiled. "So what strategies are you going to use?"

"Cut the corners!" yelled Jack.

"Keep a good rhythm," said Molly.

"Hang on tight!" said Lydia.

Everyone laughed. Donna kept whacking her whip against her boots and said nothing.

"Remember," said Jen. "You do need to go for speed, but if you cut your corners too sharply, your pony might not be able to make the jump. You don't want to risk picking up faults for a run-out or a refusal."

"Or a fall!" said Molly.

"No one," said Jen, "is going to fall. You're aiming for a fast CLEAR round. Right. Off you go. Fetch your ponies. Good luck!"

Amber mounted Beany. This time all the competitors waited quietly in the practice area, just walking their ponies around now and then to keep them occupied.

Amber looked for Dad. She knew she'd heard him cheering when she and Beany had done their clear round. She caught sight of him by the fence close to the finish. He waved, gave her the thumbs-up sign and grinned.

Amber grinned back, but her insides were turning somersaults again. She felt knotted up and nervous and very, very excited all at the same time.

She moved Beany away from the others. She needed to keep his attention. She needed to keep herself calm. She made her fingers relax on the reins, hummed to herself quietly, but found she couldn't resist turning round to see what was happening.

Lydia was approaching the last fence, or rather Silver was hurtling towards it! He completely ignored Lydia's attempts to slow him down, took off late and clattered the near rail. It fell instantly. Lydia looked so disappointed. Four faults.

"You did well," said Jen, as she rode out. Lydia tried to smile.

Then it was Jack. He really went for it and brilliantly too. He could certainly handle Roger. They were a team, Amber thought. They understood each other. She caught her breath as Jack swerved Roger tightly round to face the spread. But it was too tight. Even brave Roger couldn't tackle the jump from that angle.

"Don't worry," called Jen, as Roger ran out. "Just bring him round and try again."

This time they cleared it easily, and the last. But the run-out had cost them three faults.

"I know I won't win," said Molly, moving Feather up to the start.

"Good luck!" said Amber.

She circled Beany round the practice area, keeping an eye on Molly's progress. Slow but … clear!

"Well done!" said Amber, as Molly rode over to her.

"Not very fast," said Molly, but she was still happy.

They both turned their ponies to watch Donna. She and Polka set off at speed, clearing the first three jumps as though they weren't there. Amber's heart sank. If they kept that up they were bound to win. Donna pulled Polka tightly round to approach the spread. They'll never do it, thought Amber. It's like Jack and Roger. It's too tight. But Donna had lifted her whip and brought it smartly down on Polka's back.

That was too much for Polka. Down went his head, up went his back, and with a huge buck he sent Donna flying over the jump.

Jen was there in a flash. She helped Donna up and back into the saddle. Donna wasn't hurt, but she looked very angry. There was a bit of an argument going on. Then Donna flounced away from Jen, set Polka at the jump – Amber noticed that Jen had taken her whip away – and cleared both it and the last one, no problem. Except that the fall meant eight faults.

Amber moved Beany away. She could scarcely bear to watch the next three competitors anyway. They were all competent riders, but the boy on Jester had a daredevil flair. Despite herself, Amber turned to watch him. He was like Jack, clearing the first three easily, at speed, but he took the turn towards the spread just that little bit wider, and finished clear at a cracking pace.

Amber knew he'd be hard to beat. Her heart thumped in her chest as she rode into the ring.

The bell rang. Beany needed no urging. They were over Fences 1 and 2 in a flash and turning the corner as sharply as Amber dared towards the straight at Number 3. Over, comfortably, and she was looking ahead, planning the turn so as to pass in front of the first fence, not behind, and slowing down only long enough to change legs, then swinging round the corner into canter again.

Amber wanted to shout out, it felt so good. Beany was with her all the way.

Then it happened. A child sitting close to the arena suddenly shrieked.

Beany spooked, then shot forwards to the spread. Amber tried to steady him for the take-off but it was all happening far too quickly. Beany took off late, cat-jumped and Amber fell forward onto his neck.

The crowd gasped as Beany hurtled on towards the last. Amber clung on and struggled to get back into the saddle.

All she could think of was that she mustn't fall. A fall would mean eight faults.

But she had lost both her stirrups.

Fiercely, she thrust her hands on Beany's neck and pushed herself backwards. Almost at the jump, she took control, guided him towards the centre – and sailed over.

The crowd cheered and clapped as Amber found her stirrups and brought Beany back to a walk. She leant forward to pat and re-assure him. Her legs were like jelly.

"Wow!" said the boy on Jester. "That was some round!"

But was it good enough? Clear, yes – but how fast?

In the arena Jen was writing things on her clipboard. Amber couldn't look. Everyone was hushed.

Then Jen announced the results.

"First," she called, "Amber and Beany in a time of 16.5 seconds." She smiled. "I think that's a record, ladies and gentlemen!"

Amber rode into the arena. Everything was a blur. But the red rosette was real in her hand. The boy on Jester was second and Molly was third.

"I can't believe it!" Molly kept saying.

Everyone in the jump-off received a

rosette, and then they all did a lap of honour, Amber and Beany leading the way.

Dad was there to greet her as they came out of the arena, and there, too, was Mum with Lily and Sam.

"We managed to get here just in time," said Mum. "Well done!"

"I'm so proud of you," said Dad, as he went down the yard with Amber to the stables. "I expected brilliant jumping, but I didn't expect stunts as well! Riding on his neck indeed! Jumping without stirrups!"

Amber smiled. It was hard to take it all in. She jumped off Beany and flung her arms round his neck. Then around Dad's.

"It's been some day!" she said.

"Has it?" said Dad. "You mean you've had other excitements?"

Amber grinned.

"You could say!"

JUDY MOODY
Megan McDonald

Get in the Judy Moody mood!

Bad moods, good moods, even back-to-school moods – Judy has them all! But when her new teacher gives the class a "Me" collage project, Judy has so much fun she nearly forgets to be moody!

Meet Judy, her little "bother" Stink, her best friend Rocky and her "pest" friend Frank Pearl. They're sure to put you in a very Judy Moody mood!

MAISIE MORRIS AND THE AWFUL ARKWRIGHTS
Joanna Nadin

Maisie Morris lives with her mum in a titchy turret at the top of Withering Heights Retirement Home. While Mrs Morris looks after the residents, polishing bottoms and scrubbing smalls, Maisie plays cards and learns how to quickstep with the flamboyant Loveday Pink.

But they all live in fear of the odious owners, Mr and Mrs Arkwright, who serve cabbage water for lunch, confiscate pets and cancel Christmas. Maisie is convinced that nothing less than a miracle will deal with the revolting pair.

The great thing about miracles, though, is that you never know when one is lurking round the corner…

THE NIGHT OF THE UNICORN
Jenny Nimmo

There it was: a sky full of shooting stars. They sped through the black night, winking and glistening, and although their voices were silent, Amber felt they were trying to tell her a secret.

The following morning, Amber awakes to all sorts of discoveries. Hennie, her favourite hen, has vanished; a strange white horse appears at the animal sanctuary; and Luke Benson, the unhappy new boy at school, confides in Amber his impossible wish. But perhaps what Luke is looking for is not so far out of reach. For it suddenly seems that anything might happen…

Young readers will love this magical story by a Smarties Book Prize winner.

THE PENGUIN EXPEDITION
Jed Mercurio

Antarctica, once the coldest place on earth, is getting hotter. While some of the penguin colony, like Dude the lifeguard and the beautiful Amelia, are enjoying the sun and surf, Scott and his genius friend Humboldt discover that Penguinville is melting into the sea. Their only hope is for Scott to follow in the footsteps of his grandfather, the legendary explorer Shackleton Flipper, and lead an expedition to the South Pole to find a new and colder place to live. Follow Scott and his friends on their dangerous, exciting and entertaining adventure.